RUNNING SCARED

SIT, STAY, SLEEP COZY MYSTERIES
BOOK 4

PATTI BENNING

SUMMER PRESCOTT BOOKS PUBLISHING

Copyright 2025 Summer Prescott Books

All Rights Reserved. No part of this publication nor any of the information herein may be quoted from, nor reproduced, in any form, including but not limited to: printing, scanning, photocopying, or any other printed, digital, or audio formats, without prior express written consent of the copyright holder.

**This book is a work of fiction. Any similarities to persons, living or dead, places of business, or situations past or present, is completely unintentional.

CHAPTER ONE

A foxhound bounded through the long grass at the edge of the woods, the white tip of his tail waving like a flag. Insects droned from the shade of the trees, the sound cut only by the occasional passing of a car on the state highway in front of the motel and the drove of a lawn mower in the distance.

To the foxhound, the motel and the woods surrounding it was a little slice of paradise. To Sadie Barton, his owner, the entire property was one big headache.

Today, it was giving her a stomachache, too. It was the evening of her first dog training class, and she was so nervous she hadn't been able to do more than snack on some frozen waffles and sip water all day.

She had worked as a dog trainer for years, and she

couldn't remember being this nervous—even at her very first lesson at her old training facility…but that was different. That was just a job. This was her livelihood.

Business at the motel and attached boarding kennel had picked up a little in the past couple of weeks, but the motel's reputation lingered like a stain that wouldn't come out, and many of the locals were still wary of it. Sadie couldn't blame them, not really. She wasn't sure if *she* would want to stay at a motel that had a history of killing its guests, or board her dog there—never mind the fact that she currently lived above the lobby—but that didn't mean she liked how the reputation drove away potential boarding clients or sometimes spooked their guests into leaving early when they went into town and heard about the troubles the motel had experienced.

She hoped the training class tonight would change things, or at least start to. She was keeping the roster small for her first class—just six dogs and their owners—and they were sticking to the basics. Leash manners, sit, down, stay, and recall. The class was a six-week course, and she was giving a steep discount for her first clients. She and Penny, her best friend and business partner, needed the money, but they needed good reviews and a solid client base more.

She stepped back from the freshly mown grassy area behind the motel where she was hosting the lesson and put her hands on her hips as she surveyed the half-circle of folding chairs she had set up. She had also dragged out a folding table, which held water bottles, dog treats, and a stack of informational pamphlets she had printed off earlier that day. In the shade underneath it, a big bowl of cool water waited for the dogs.

It wasn't anything fancy. She had dreams of one day building a pole barn on the property, which she could use as a proper training facility, but for now she was going to have to make do. At least the temperature and humidity were bearable. It was mid-October, and the days no longer felt like they were trying to smother her. She was desperate enough to be grateful for even the smallest of mercies.

Jasper, her two-and-a-half-year-old rescued foxhound, trotted over to her, his pink tongue hanging from the side of his mouth. As he checked in with her, she leaned down to run her hands over his short coat, checking for any ticks that might have hitched a ride. He was on a preventative, but it didn't stop them from crawling on him when he ran through the tall grass. When she finished, he trotted away to lap up water from the bowl under the table.

"Save some for our guests, buddy," she said, patting her leg to call him back over. The lesson area was as prepared as it was going to get and she still had a good half an hour before her clients were supposed to arrive—just enough time to go in, change into something a little more presentable, and check in with Penny.

Jasper trotted ahead of her as they walked around the side of the motel. Sam, their surprise tenant who lived in the little yellow house that was attached to the property, was just finishing up mowing the lawn on his big riding mower. Normally, she and Penny took turns hacking away at the grass with the old push mower he had given them, but they didn't have time to do that today, and she wanted the place to look nice for her training clients.

She had offered to pay him, but Sam refused the cash. She felt bad, because she knew his lawn care business was how he made a living. She didn't want him to feel like he had to take care of the motel's yard for free just because they were his landlords.

She would have to figure out how to properly thank him another day, though, because right now all she could think about was how many ways tonight's class could go wrong. She raised a hand to wave at him as he turned the mower around to do another strip, and he waved back. She was glad he couldn't see how sweaty her palms were from this distance. She wiped them on her jean shorts before she continued around to the front of the motel.

Jasper was already waiting by the door and slipped inside as she opened it. He trotted directly over to his own water bowl in the corner and continued drinking, while Sadie went over to the front desk, where Penny was busy printing out flyers for the boarding kennel. They were running a new deal—if someone boarded two dogs from the same household, they would take the second dog at half their usual price.

Marketing was one thing Sadie never had to worry about when she was working at someone else's kennel, and she hadn't realized just how much of a time sink it would be. They were desperate for clients, so it wasn't something they could neglect, but Sadie held out hope that one day she would be able to let someone else deal with all of that, so her only focus would be the dogs.

"Is everything set up?" Penny asked, glancing up from the printer.

"I think so," Sadie said. "At least the weather is nice today."

If it was raining, she would have to host the lesson

in the lobby. It would be cramped, and they would face potential distractions if a guest came in during the lesson.

"Sorry I didn't help set up," Penny said. "I'll come help you clean everything up when it's done."

"That's fine, you had stuff to do in here," Sadie said. "Did the person we were going to put in Room Two ever check in?"

"They did," Penny said. "A nice, older woman and some sort of fluffy little mutt. I told her about our daycare service and she said she might think about it if she ends up going out to eat with a friend while she's here, so that's something."

"Oh, good," Sadie said. She looked around their lobby, which was pretty bare bones at the moment. "We should get a little table to feature advertisements from local businesses and whatever tourist attractions we can find in the area. That might encourage people to go out and do stuff, which would then encourage them to pay for us to watch their dogs."

"That's a good idea," Penny said.

She tapped the space bar on her laptop to wake it up and quickly made a note. They had a running list of ideas that might help bring in more business. At this point, they were desperate enough to try almost anything.

"I'm going to run upstairs and get changed," Sadie said. "If someone shows up early, can you send them around back?"

Penny nodded. Calling Jasper to come with her, Sadie unlocked the door that led to the stairs up to her apartment. The little one-bedroom apartment above the lobby was cramped and somehow still smelled like potpourri, but it was cozy enough.

Living at the same place where she worked made her feel like she never had any time off, but she liked being there overnight so she could react quickly if there was a problem with one of the dogs that she was boarding, and it was a good idea to have someone around at all times whenever they had guests anyway.

For the time being, Penny had it worse: she was living out of one of their motel rooms. She was planning to find an apartment or a small house to rent in town as soon as they had enough regular income for her to afford it, but, for now, it was a free place to live, and it wasn't as if they needed the room for guests—they hadn't gone a single night without at least one vacancy so far.

Sadie got changed quickly, putting on a pair of khaki capris and a clean t-shirt. She pulled her hair back into a tight ponytail and took a look in the mirror to make sure she looked presentable, if not fancy. No one would be expecting her to be dressed in formal business attire for a dog training class, but she didn't want to come across as a slob either.

Satisfied with her appearance, she turned her attention to Jasper and quickly wiped a few grass stains from the white parts of his coat before she clipped a leash to his collar and led him back downstairs, pausing to grab a folded-up blanket on her way out.

He was going to be her demo dog for the lesson, but even if she didn't need him to help her demonstrate what she wanted her clients to do, she would have wanted him with her anyway. She was so nervous that she felt lightheaded, and he was a calming presence beside her.

No one had arrived yet, but that was fine. There were still fifteen minutes before the lesson was supposed to start. She spent those minutes pacing in the lobby, pausing every few steps to peer out the window. Five minutes to six, she saw a familiar vehicle pull into the parking lot. Taking a deep breath, Sadie opened the lobby door. She paused to thank Penny for her "Good luck," then stepped outside.

Beth and Rosco had arrived. They were her first regular boarding clients—Beth boarded Rosco with them almost every weekend—and Beth had been the first person to sign up for her training classes, too. She smiled and waved at the older woman, then led Jasper across the parking lot to greet them. He and Rosco were good pals by now, so they let the dogs say hi before Sadie led Beth behind the building to where the folding chairs waited.

One down, five more people to go before her lesson could begin.

CHAPTER TWO

Four more of her training clients arrived in the next few minutes. Sadie waited until ten minutes after six, but the last one, a man by the name of Michael Kingsley, who had a hound mix named Loki, didn't arrive, and finally she decided to start the class without him.

It was a little disappointing that one of her clients had decided to ghost her, but five wasn't a bad turnout for her very first lesson. She paused for a moment to survey the group. There was Rosco, who was a young lab mix, a Bernese Mountain Dog, some sort of scruffy terrier mix, a Basset Hound, and a Pit Bull mix.

Beth was the only owner she knew well, so she took a minute to go around and introduce herself to everyone else and greet their dogs while Jasper lay on the folded blanket opposite the chairs. Jasper was the sort of dog who loved everyone, human and animal alike, but she knew not all dogs felt the same way. She had specifically only taken clients that didn't have major aggression issues for her first lesson, but just because they were okay with other dogs at a distance didn't mean they would appreciate her overly friendly foxhound invading their space.

As soon as all of her clients had introduced themselves, and the people and dogs were mostly settled, Sadie stepped back to stand next to Jasper and took a deep breath.

"Thanks for coming, everyone. Let's get started."

The class was an hour long, but they went a little late since she had started it late. The first lesson was an introductory one so she could get a feel for what each of the dogs needed and what the owners hoped to achieve during the class. Walking nicely on a leash was one thing they all struggled with, so at the end of the first lesson, she gave them all homework: they each needed to practice loose leash walking for at least ten minutes a day between now and the next lesson. She wanted them to go somewhere with few distractions where they could take their time to only walk when their dog wasn't pulling. If the dog pulled, they were to take a few steps back and use a treat or toy to get the dog's attention until the dog was focused on them again.

The goal was for the dogs to learn that pulling didn't get them anywhere, but keeping the leash slack and focusing on their owner did.

It was a simple lesson, but she thought everyone had a good time. A few of her clients even offered to stay and help her clean up, but she thanked them and told them it wasn't necessary.

Beth was the last to go. She lingered to talk to Sadie briefly before leaving.

"I just wanted to say thank you for the lovely lesson," she said. "I'm going to work with Rosco every day, just like you said. I would love for him to be able to start coming with me when I visit my daughter and granddaughter, but he needs more manners before he can be around the baby. Being able to walk him without him pulling will be a great start. I swear, he almost yanks my arm out of its socket every day."

"Well, this method will work, but it might take some time," Sadie said. "He's still a young dog and he's full of energy. Once he learns the concept of having some restraint and self-control, it should translate into other areas of his training as well. Feel free to call me if you have any questions or need help with anything before the next lesson."

She stood at the edge of the parking lot and waved as Beth loaded Rosco into her car and pulled away. Her nerves had settled just a few minutes after beginning the lesson, and she felt overall positive about how things had gone. Everyone seemed happy, and she thought the dogs had a good time. She was already looking forward to next week's lesson. Eventually, she wanted to have multiple classes each week, but for now she was content to take things slow to make sure she didn't get overwhelmed or exhaust her client base. She hoped many of her current clients would move on to more advanced classes once they finished this one.

She returned to the training area to grab her first armful of stuff from the table and carried it into the lobby, Jasper at her heels. She let him in first, then followed behind him. Penny looked up from the desk.

"How'd it go?"

"I think it went really well," Sadie said. "Did a Michael Kingsley call to cancel? He didn't show up to the lesson."

"No, we didn't get any calls," Penny said. She looked confused for a moment, then her expression slowly changed to worry. "Hold on, I saw an alert when I was online."

"An alert?" Sadie dumped the empty water bottles into the garbage and put the unopened ones on the front desk before walking around to join Penny behind it as she typed on her computer.

"Yeah, it was in the town's group on social media. Let's see…"

She scrolled down the page until she found what she was looking for and clicked to open the post.

Fatal crash on Wildermuth Road, be on lookout for loose dog.

Sadie's stomach dropped as soon as she read the headline. Penny scrolled down so they could look through the comments, but no one seemed to know who the victim was yet. The fact that there was a dog involved was too much of a coincidence for her to ignore, though.

"Where are you going?" Penny asked as Sadie turned toward the door to her apartment.

"I'm going to get my purse. I want to drive out there and see what's going on."

"Do you think it might be the guy who didn't show up?"

"I don't know," Sadie said. "But even if it's not, maybe I could help with the dog. People drive way too fast out here, and I hate the thought of any dog wandering loose in these woods."

It wasn't just cars the dog had to worry about, either. There was dangerous wildlife, too. Even if the dog didn't belong to one of her clients, she still wanted to help if she could.

"I'll come with you," Penny said, rising from her chair.

Sadie hesitated, then shook her head. "No, you should stay here. We have a couple of guests, and there's two dogs boarding in the kennel. It doesn't feel right leaving them without anyone here."

Penny slowly lowered back into her chair, frowning. "Then you should ask Sam to go with you. We have no idea what even happened. What if you find the dog, but it's aggressive or hurt or something? There could be people at the scene who are upset, too."

"I'll send him a text," Sadie promised. She patted her leg to call Jasper over, then started up to her apartment.

She hoped the victim wasn't Michael, and that the loose dog had been caught already, but in her gut, she knew they had discovered what had happened to her missing client.

CHAPTER THREE

She sent Sam a text message as soon as she reached the top of the stairs up to her apartment. She made sure Jasper was settled with a fresh bowl of water and his dinner in case she was out late, and kissed him on top of his furry head before heading back down to the lobby.

Sam had responded by the time she rejoined Penny. Her own message had been a confused jumble of words.

Hey, I think one of my clients got into a car accident and now their dog is running loose on Wildermuth Road. I want to go check it out, but Penny doesn't think I should go alone. Do you have time to come with me and see what's going on?

His reply was simple; *Yes.*

She checked in with Penny to see if there had been any updates on what had happened or if anyone had released the victim's name yet, but there hadn't been. Her friend got up to give her a worried hug.

"Keep me updated. I hope you find the dog, no matter whose it is."

"I'll let you know what's going on when I get there," Sadie said, "and thanks. So do I."

She left through the lobby door, her keys in her hand. She was prepared to go over to Sam's house to pick him up, but he was already walking over from the narrow path that led between the motel and his house. She waved when she saw him, then got into her SUV and started the engine. He got into the passenger side a few moments later, already typing in his phone. He held it up so she could see the screen before she backed out of the parking space.

What happened?

Sam was mute. He had been teaching her some simple signs, but mostly he communicated with her by writing in a notebook or typing on his phone. He could make his phone read text if she couldn't look away from what she was doing, which was convenient even if it was a bit strange to chat with a robotic voice.

She still didn't know why he either couldn't or

didn't speak, and it didn't seem like the sort of thing she could just come out and ask him. Regardless of the occasional difficulties, they managed to get by all right, and she was glad he was coming with her today, even if they couldn't chat quite as easily as she and Penny could while she was driving.

"I had six people signed up for the class tonight," she explained as she turned onto the main road. "Only five turned up."

She thought she vaguely remembered seeing a sign for Wildermuth Road by the gas station a few miles away, though she didn't know which part of the road the accident had happened on. She turned away from town and sped up, glad for once that the stretch of the highway wasn't normally very busy, even though if it had been, they probably would have gotten more guests.

"After the class ended, Penny said she saw a post online about a fatal car accident and a loose dog on Wildermuth Road," she continued. "They haven't released any names yet, but it seems like too much of a coincidence to ignore. Even if it isn't the guy who didn't show up to the lesson, I'd still like to help catch the dog if I can."

Other than a feed store, a vet clinic, and another small boarding kennel about twenty minutes away, hers was the only dedicated pet-related business in town. She felt like that gave her a responsibility to help animals when she could, and at least if she found the dog and couldn't get in touch with the owners right away, she was set up to keep the dog safe and comfortable at the kennel until she could figure out who to return it to. Someone else might have no option other than to take it to the county animal shelter, which she hadn't heard anything good about.

Sam nodded, his jaw tight with concern. She realized that he very well might know the person who had been involved in the accident. He had grown up in Greencreek and knew a lot of the locals, even if just by name. She and Penny still didn't know very many people in town, so she felt a little detached from the whole thing. It was a tragedy, of course, and she felt horrible for everyone who was involved in the accident and their families, but it didn't feel personal to her in the same way it would if it was someone she knew.

She made a right turn when she reached a stop sign at the intersection and kept her eyes peeled for the Wildermuth Road sign. Sam was the one who pointed it out to her. She hit her blinker and turned toward town, assuming that was the most likely direction the vehicle had been coming from, especially if it really was her client and he had been on his way to the motel when the accident happened.

If she had the timing right, the accident would have been nearly an hour and a half ago, which meant it was possible the emergency responders had already come and gone.

"There might not even be anything to see," she said as she drove down the tree-lined road. "I figure we can turn around once we reach—"

She broke off mid-sentence and slammed the brakes when something large and white with black splotches ran across the road in front of them. The dog passed just inches in front of her car. She saw blue ticking in its white fur, a telltale sign that this was a hound mix… just like the dog Michael Kingsley was supposed to bring to class.

She had the foresight to hit her hazards as she put her SUV into park and jumped out of the vehicle. The dog was already in the trees on the far side of the road. It took one look back at her, then took off running. She whistled and clapped her hands and called out, "Here, doggie, come here!" but it vanished into the trees without looking back.

Shaken from the near-miss, she turned back to her car to get the bag of treats she kept on the back seat, but Sam had already grabbed them and walked around the SUV to hand them to her. She smiled at him in thanks, then shook the bag, hoping the crinkling sound would draw the dog's attention.

"Hey, did you see a dog running loose around here?"

She looked up at the man's voice and saw someone jogging down the shoulder of the road toward them. He had short blond hair and was wearing tracksuit pants and a loose tank top.

"We did," she said. "He looked like a hound mix."

"That's the dog I'm looking for," he said. "Did he look injured?"

"No, but we almost hit him," Sadie said. "It was a close thing. Are you the owner?"

"No, not quite," he said. He slowed to walk the rest of the distance over to them and held out his hand to shake with her. "I'm Landon Bellows, his previous owner. The dog's name is Loki. His current owner was, unfortunately, killed in a car accident earlier this evening. The dog was in the vehicle at the time and, from what I can figure out, he panicked and took off running after the accident happened."

Loki was the name of the dog who was supposed to come to her lesson today. She swallowed. She already knew the answer, but she still had to be sure. "Was the current owner's name Michael Kingsley?"

Landon's eyebrows rose. "That's him. Did you know him?"

"No," she said. "Not exactly. I'm Sadie Barton, and I own the motel on Highway 78. I think he and Loki were on the way to a dog training class I'm hosting when the accident happened. They never showed up, and I saw a post about the accident when the class ended. I saw that there was a loose dog, and I figured I'd come out here to try to help catch it. Do you know what caused the accident?"

"I don't," Landon said. "I just got here ten or fifteen minutes ago. Michael's wife, Ginny, called me to see if I'd be willing to help catch Loki. She thought since he knew me, he might be willing to come to me even though he's scared. She would do it herself, but she's still dealing with the police, and I think she's going to be a little too distraught to get back out here this evening."

"I can imagine," Sadie said. "I feel terrible for her."

"Did you see which way he went?" Landon asked. "I'm hoping once he catches my smell, he'll come when I call. Poor guy must be terrified."

"He went that way," she said, pointing into the woods. "Here, if you think he'll come to the treats, you can take the bag."

"Thanks," Landon said. He accepted the bag of treats from her and looked both ways before jogging across the road. He paused on the other side and turned back toward them to call out, "I don't know if he'll come to you since he doesn't know you, but you're welcome to try. We can use all the help we can get. The next car might not stop in time."

CHAPTER FOUR

Since Landon was chasing after Loki, and there was a good chance that the presence of more people would just frighten the dog further, she and Sam got back into the SUV. She decided to continue on toward town, to see whether anyone was still at the site of the accident. She knew Wildermuth Road led back to Main Street, so essentially they would be driving in a big loop that would eventually take them back to Highway 78 and the motel.

They passed a car parked along the side of the road about a mile up from where they left—she assumed it was his car. The site of the accident was a few miles further up the road. She saw the sheriff's vehicle parked along the shoulder of the road behind the accident, its lights flashing, and a dark purple minivan was parked behind it. Someone had put up orange cones to close the lane, and there was a tow truck parked along the shoulder in front of the accident.

Michael's vehicle was off the road, in the ditch, the hood crumpled where it had hit a tree and the driver's side panel dented in as if something had collided with it. Broken glass littered the road, and a shape under a white sheet lay in the grass alongside the shoulder. She didn't look too closely at the latter as she parked the SUV along the opposite shoulder so they could get a better look at the scene. She told herself she just wanted to see how bad the accident was, in order to judge whether Loki might be injured. That felt like a better excuse than rubbernecking.

"Did you know him?" she asked Sam as they stared at the accident. "Michael Kingsley, I mean."

He shook his head. That was a small relief. Even though she had suspected he was the one involved in the accident, it was still hard to wrap her head around the fact that one of her very first dog training clients had died on their way to her first ever lesson.

She knew it wasn't rational, but she couldn't shake the feeling of guilt. If she hadn't scheduled the lesson for *this* time on *this* day, Michael might still be alive. Of course, there was no way she could have possibly known something like this would happen, but it still didn't sit right with her.

Sheriff Islington was standing near the hood of his car speaking to a middle-aged woman who was half sitting on the sheriff's car's hood, dabbing at her eyes with a tissue. She didn't look up when they parked, but the sheriff did. After a second, he crossed the road and she lowered her window.

"Evening, Sadie," he said. Even though they had only been in the area for a couple of months, he was unfortunately familiar with both her and Penny. They'd had a streak of bad luck at the motel. She'd thought it was over, but now she wasn't so sure. The sheriff peered into the vehicle, taking in Sam without comment, before asking, "No Penny today?"

"No, she stayed at the motel," Sadie said.

He nodded. For a brief second, she thought he looked disappointed, but his expression quickly shifted into something more professional.

"Mind if I ask what y'all are doing here? I usually tell people to move on if they stop to ogle at a crime scene, but you don't seem the type."

"I read about the accident online," she explained. "The man who died, Michael Kingsley, he was supposed to come to a dog training class at the motel earlier, but he never showed up. I saw that there was a loose dog, too, and I thought I'd come out here to see if I could help catch it. We just saw the dog cross the road a couple miles back, but someone named Landon was already chasing after him."

The sheriff nodded. "That makes sense. The victim's wife mentioned he was on his way to a dog training class, though she didn't say where. I should have guessed it was at your motel."

Behind him, she saw the woman—she assumed this was Michael's wife, Ginny—rise from her seat on the hood of the car and start over toward them. The sheriff turned to follow her gaze and stepped back to wave her over.

"Virginia," he said with a nod.

"What's going on?" she asked. Her eyes were puffy and red-rimmed, and her voice shook, but she looked at them like she was ready for a confrontation. "What are these people doing here?"

"This is Sadie Barton and Sam Walker," the sheriff said. "Your husband was on his way to the dog training class Ms. Barton was hosting at her motel. When he never showed up, she got worried about him and checked online, where she saw the post about his accident. She came out here to help catch the dog."

Immediately, the woman's expression softened. "Oh, that's so kind of you," she said. "He loved that dog. I just can't imagine losing both of them at once like this. I feel horrible. This is all my fault."

"Nonsense," the sheriff said. "You can't blame yourself for this."

"It *was*," Ginny said. "I'm the one who begged him to take the dog to a training class. He would never have signed up for it if it wasn't for me."

"It was an accident," Sadie said gently. "No one could have guessed this would happen."

"It wasn't an accident," the other woman replied, her voice sharp. "Someone murdered him." Her voice broke on the last two words, and she turned away to sob into her hands.

The sheriff patted his pockets, then leaned over toward Sadie and whispered, "Y'all wouldn't happen to have a tissue, would you?"

She didn't, but she had a bundle of clean napkins from a fast food restaurant tucked into the door pocket, which she handed to him.

He took a few from the stack and handed them over to Ginny, who blew her nose.

"It wasn't an accident?" Sadie asked hesitantly.

She didn't want to pry into what was obviously a source of pain and grief for the other woman, but it seemed like an important fact to get straight, especially if she was going to keep helping look for Loki.

"Unfortunately, no," the sheriff said. He hesitated, then cleared his throat. "Virginia, why don't you go sit in your vehicle? Or if you want, you're free to head on home. Your sister's coming to stay with you, is that correct?"

Ginny nodded, still dabbing at tears from her eyes. "I don't want to go back yet," she said. "Not until they take him away." Her voice wavered. "I want to say goodbye to him one last time when the coroner arrives."

"You'll get your chance," the sheriff promised, his voice gentle. "If you need anything, you just honk or shout out the window. Remember, I've got water in the cruiser, and I'm sure I could dig up a snack for you if you get hungry. Whatever will keep you comfortable."

"I don't think I'll ever be hungry again," she muttered.

He handed her the rest of the napkins, and she trudged across the road. The sheriff waited until she was seated in her van with the door shut before he turned back to them.

"I didn't want to talk about it in front of her," the sheriff said. "She already knows what happened, but there's no sense in making her hear it all again. From what I can tell, it looks like someone struck the vehicle from the side and caused it to go off the road. That *could* have been an accident, though it would have been a hit and run and still a crime since the perpetrator didn't stop or call for help. What makes me so sure this was a homicide is the fact that the driver's side window was broken open and the victim was found in the ditch a few feet away from his car with significant head injuries that I wouldn't expect from an accident like this. I believe someone ran him off the road intentionally and then killed him with blunt trauma to the head, either when he tried to escape the vehicle or when he was forcibly removed from the vehicle by the killer. We're keeping the details quiet, and I'd appreciate it if you'd keep this to yourselves for now, but if you're going to help look for that dog, you ought to know what you're getting into. It's likely that this was a targeted attack, and the killer may attempt to go after other parties who are connected to Michael Kingsley, including his wife or even his dog."

"I see," Sadie said. "Thank you for telling me. We'll keep it quiet."

She looked over at Sam for confirmation, but he wasn't paying attention. He was staring at the minivan instead. She followed his gaze and immediately realized what he was looking at.

The van had damage to the front bumper. One corner of it was crumpled in, and there were scratches in the paint as if it had hit something big. Sam glanced at her and they exchanged a look.

Ginny's grief seemed real, but was it possible they were crocodile tears? Had she run her own husband off the road?

CHAPTER FIVE

"Y'all think you'll have any luck catching that dog?"

Sadie forced her attention back to the sheriff. He must have noticed the damage on Ginny's car, and he must have already asked her about it. She should trust his judgment—if he didn't think it was concerning, then neither should she.

"I'll do my best," she said, not wanting to drag Sam into it. "There's someone else out there looking for him. A guy named Landon who said he was Loki's previous owner. I'm hoping he'll be able to catch the dog this evening. But if not, I'll do what I can to get him to safety."

"You'll need Virginia's number, in case you do catch the mutt," he said. "I'm sure she'll appreciate the help. Poor woman's got enough on her plate already. I've got it written down somewhere here." He patted his pocket and took a notebook out.

"I can just go ask her for it myself," she said. "That way I can give her my number too, so she can let me know if someone else catches Loki."

She didn't say it, but she also wanted another chance to talk to the woman after seeing that damage to her van.

"Suit yourself," Sheriff Islington said. "I'm going to go check on the status of that coroner. Y'all are free to take off once you're done here."

Sadie unbuckled her seatbelt as the sheriff walked away. "I'll be right back," she said to Sam as she opened the door.

She paused to check for oncoming traffic, then jogged across the road and passed the orange cones as she walked to the van. When Ginny saw her approaching, she rolled down her window.

"Yes?"

"The sheriff suggested that we trade numbers so I can let you know if I catch Loki, and you can let me know if someone else gets him so I don't come back out here for nothing."

"Oh, I should have thought of that," she said. She took out her cell phone and looked at Sadie expectantly. Sadie recited her number and Virginia typed it in, then said, "I'll send you a text message so you have mine. It's very kind of you to help."

"It's my job, sort of," Sadie said.

She glanced down at the damage to the car. She didn't want to bring it up directly, but she was curious. Ginny must have seen where she looked because her expression became closed off.

"I'll tell you the same thing I told Sheriff Islington. That damage was already there long before today. You can verify it with Ben Stanford at the auto shop. I took it in to get a quote last week. I loved my husband. I didn't do this."

Sadie apologized, even though she hadn't technically said anything. She thanked Ginny for her number before promising once again to do everything she could to get Loki to safety.

She jogged back across the street and got into her SUV, where she told Sam about Ginny's claim that her van was already damaged as she buckled her seatbelt.

She turned around in the road and headed back the direction they had come from. A mile down, she spotted Landon walking back to his car empty-handed and slowed her vehicle. As they drew even with him, she rolled down the passenger side window so she could call out to him across Sam.

"Any luck?"

Landon shook his head. He looked dejected. "No, I got close to him once, but he took off running when I called for him. The accident must have really spooked him. It's getting too dark to see properly in the woods now, but I'll be back out here tomorrow."

"I'll come back tomorrow, too," she said. "I might see if I can find a live trap big enough to catch him. If you get the chance, you could leave some clothes with a familiar scent on them, either yours or Ginny's or Michael's. Having a familiar, comforting smell might draw him back to the area."

"That's a good idea," Landon said. "I've got an old sweatshirt in the car. I'll leave it tied to a tree or something before I head out. Thanks for all your help."

"I'm happy to do it," she said. "I won't be able to sleep knowing there's a lost dog out here, even if he isn't mine."

She rolled up the window and began to pull away, but at the last second, she slowed again and glanced in the rearview mirror at Landon's car. It was a stormy, metallic gray color she rather liked. More importantly, there wasn't a scrape on it.

Reassured, she pulled away and got up to speed. She knew she was going to be checking for damage on people's vehicles for a long time to come. She suspected the sheriff was right and Michael had been targeted. It didn't make any sense that a stranger would run someone's car off the road and then go so far as to murder the victim for no reason. This felt personal, and if it was personal, it meant the culprit was likely to be a local.

She and Sam rode the rest of the way back to the motel in silence, though when they arrived, they sat in the parking lot for a few minutes to chat.

Do you need me to go back out there with you tomorrow? he wrote in his notebook.

"I don't think so," she said. "I'm going to stop at the hardware store in the morning to see if they sell live traps big enough, and if they do, I'm just going to go out and set it up a few feet into the woods, right off the road. I think having too many people out there might spook him. If he won't even come to Landon, he probably won't come to me."

I'll keep an eye out for him when I'm driving around, he wrote. *I'll let you know if I see him.*

"Thanks, Sam," she said. "I know it probably seems ridiculous for me to be this worried about a dog I haven't even met, but he was supposed to be one of my training clients. I meant what I said to Landon: I'd be worried about any dog that's out there alone. He must be so scared after what happened, especially now that he's all alone in those thick woods at night." She sighed and looked down at her steering wheel. "I wish I'd scheduled the lesson for any other day."

After a second, Sam nudged her. She looked up to see him holding up his notebook. *You couldn't have known. How did the lesson go?*

"It went really well," she admitted. "I think everyone was satisfied, and I'm looking forward to next week despite…everything. Thanks again for mowing. I know Penny and I should be better at keeping up with it."

It's a lot of lawn to handle with just a push mower, he wrote. *It doesn't take long to do on the riding mower, though. I don't mind keeping it up for you.*

"We definitely want to hire you as soon as we can afford it," she said. "Until then, we'll just keep hacking away at it ourselves unless there's another lawn care emergency like there was yesterday." She unbuckled her seatbelt. "I should get going. I'm sure Penny wants an update. I forgot to text her when we got there."

I'll see you around, he wrote.

"Yeah. Goodnight, Sam."

They got out of her SUV and she waved as he

walked away toward the path between the motel and his house before she turned toward the lobby. She still had to take care of the two dogs that were boarding with them and send updates to their owners, but after that, her day would be done and she would finally get a chance to rest.

CHAPTER SIX

The very first thing Sadie did on Thursday morning, before she even got out of bed, was send a text message to Ginny asking if Loki had been found yet. By the time she finished feeding Jasper and the two boarding dogs, Ginny had replied.

I haven't heard anything yet. I think Landon is the last one who saw him yesterday evening. Please let me know if you spot him when you go out!

Sadie promised she would, then slipped her phone into the pocket of her scrubs and shoved her feet into a pair of rubber boots so she could begin cleaning the kennels. When she was done, she waited for the kennels to dry before she let the dogs back in and made sure everyone had fresh water and clean bedding.

She left Jasper in the last run, since she didn't want to bring him with her while she was looking for Loki, then went back upstairs to get changed into jeans and a t-shirt. She traded her rubber boots for a pair of hiking shoes, and grabbed one of Jasper's spare slip leads and another bag of dog treats in case she got lucky and saw Loki while she was setting up the trap.

If she could even find a trap that was large enough. She didn't remember seeing them at the hardware store in town, but then she hadn't exactly been looking, either. It was worth a try. Worst case scenario, she lost out on half an hour of her morning with nothing to show for it.

Penny was busy doing a load of laundry when she went back downstairs. She popped into the laundry room to chat with her before leaving.

"I'm heading into town," she said. "Do you want me to grab anything?"

"I don't think so," Penny said. "I just made one of those microwave scrambled egg bowls for breakfast or I'd ask for something from the diner. It's probably best to save my money, anyway. Are you going to look for that dog?"

"I'm going to stop at the hardware store first," Sadie explained. "I need to see if they have a live trap big enough for him. After that, I'm going to stop where I saw him last on Wildermuth Road and either set up the trap or head out to look for him. I won't be gone for more than a couple hours, so if you want to take a break later, you can."

"Thanks. I don't think we'll be that busy today, but it might be nice to get out of here for a while. I know there isn't much to do around here most days, but it's still been wearing on me to never have a real day off."

"Hopefully by this time next year, we'll be doing well enough to hire a couple of employees," Sadie said. "That's the dream, anyway."

She said a final goodbye and backed out of the laundry room, then turned to walk out of the lobby door. She nearly ran into Sam, who had a paper bag in one hand and his notebook in the other.

"Sorry, I wasn't expecting anyone to be out here," she said as she caught herself from stumbling into him.

He waved her apology off, then held up the notebook, which held a pre-written message on it.

I dug a couple of trail cams out of storage. Thought you could use them to check for that dog. They're solar powered, and you can download the images from your phone if you're close enough for the bluetooth to connect, so you don't have to worry about fiddling with SD cards or batteries.

She took the bag and peered into it, seeing two camouflaged trail cams, complete with straps.

"Wow, thanks, Sam," she said. "These are great. I'll set them up around where we saw Loki yesterday. Hopefully he's still in the area. Ginny says she doesn't think anyone's spotted him since Landon was out there yesterday evening."

She briefly thought about asking Sam to come with her into town, but decided that might be a strange request to make. She didn't actually *need* someone to come with her today, and it wasn't an emergency situation like yesterday had been.

He was their tenant, and she was his landlord—she didn't want him to feel obligated to hang out with her. It wasn't his fault she didn't have any friends in town other than Penny.

She got into her SUV, setting the trail cams on the passenger seat floorboard. She checked behind her before she backed up to make sure Sam was out of the way, but he was already halfway down the path back to his house. She was touched by the trail cam gesture. It meant he was thinking about Loki. She always liked it when other people showed empathy toward animals. In her experience, it was a red flag if they didn't care.

She made the now-familiar drive into Greencreek and parked along the curb in front of the hardware store. She could see Norma's familiar white head of hair through the window. The elderly woman who owned the hardware store had employees who worked most weekends, but she was almost always there by herself during the week.

As she got out of her vehicle, she wondered whether she and Penny would own the motel long enough for their hair to go as white as Norma's. As much as she hated to admit it out loud, buying the motel had been something of an impulse decision that they made just weeks after both of their boyfriends showed their true colors—Penny's by living a double life and cheating on her, and her own by covering for him.

The motel and kennel business had been an escape into fantasy after the trauma of losing both of their partners in one fell swoop, and the reality of it was a lot more difficult than Sadie had expected. She had been wanting to open her own boarding kennel and training business for years, but in her dreams, clients poured in effortlessly. In real life, each one was a struggle to get.

Truth be told, she wasn't even sure if she *wanted* to spend the rest of her life in Greencreek. It was a far cry from Lexington, where she had grown up. She didn't mind it for now—living in such a small town was a different experience, and it was fun being on an adventure like this with her best friend—but she wasn't sure if she would feel the same in five or ten years.

It wasn't something they had to decide right now. Their first priority, no matter what the future held, was getting the motel to be profitable. As long as it was a successful business, they could always sell it if they wanted to move somewhere else, but if it wasn't profitable, then the more money they sank into it, the more they stood to lose.

Finding Loki wouldn't do anything to help the business other than perhaps giving them a small boost of reputation, but that wasn't why she was doing this. She was doing it for the dog's own well-being and for Ginny, who had already lost so much.

She walked into the hardware store, locking her SUV behind her. Norma turned toward her with a smile when the bell over the door rang.

"Hello, dear," she said. "What can I help you with today?"

"I'm looking for a live trap big enough for a large

dog," Sadie said. "Do you have something like that in stock?"

"Hmm, let's see," Norma said.

She left her place behind the register, and Sadie followed her down a narrow aisle. Norma led her all the way to the back, where Sadie saw a shelving unit full of various types of traps, but the largest one she saw was only big enough to fit a raccoon.

"I could have sworn we had some of the big ones left," Norma said. "They aren't very popular. I might have moved them off the floor to make room for something else. Let's see…"

She walked into the corner and opened a swinging door that led to the back. Sadie hesitated, but the older woman gestured for her to follow.

Much like the rest of the store, the storeroom was absolutely packed full of merchandise. The hardware store was really more like a general store. It sold everything except for fresh produce, and it was essential to the community in a way the motel would never be. She wished they had decided to invest in something like this.

Well, not really. It might be a steadier type of business, but she knew there would always be a part of her that wanted to work with dogs instead. At least now, she could tell herself she had chased her dream, even if the motel ended up failing.

"Will this do?" Norma asked, drawing Sadie's attention to a large wire live trap in the corner. "It's the only one I have left. I'll let it go to you at a discount. These things take up so much space, and they're expensive to ship, too. I don't think I'll be getting any more in."

"That's perfect," Sadie said. "How much?"

She walked out of the hardware store nearly a hundred dollars lighter, and wrangled the live trap into the back of the SUV. It was a lot of money to spend, especially when things were so tight, but it would be worth it if it helped her catch Loki. Maybe she could return it after—but Norma seemed happy to get rid of it, and she didn't want to do anything to sour their relationship with the elderly owner of the hardware store.

She got into her vehicle and started the engine, then checked her phone to make sure there hadn't been any updates from Ginny. Nothing, which meant that Loki was still out there. She bit the inside of her cheek as she reread Ginny's last message.

The damage to the other woman's vehicle still bothered her. It seemed like too much of a coincidence, and didn't the statistics say that the victim's spouse was often the primary suspect in a homicide case? She didn't want to undermine Sheriff Islington, but she had to be sure if she was going to be working with Ginny to find her dog—and she didn't want Loki to go back into the hands of a killer, either.

She glanced at her SUV's dashboard and fiddled with her trip counter until it showed how long it had been since her last oil change. She was just about due for another one. It would be a good excuse to go to that auto shop Ginny had mentioned and see if she could at least figure out who this Ben guy was and get a feel for him.

Even if he verified her story, he could be lying. Ginny could have paid him off to twist the truth. She wouldn't have much more to go on than her gut feeling, but if he seemed honest, then she would feel a little better about the whole situation.

And if he seemed dishonest…well, she would cross that bridge if she came to it.

CHAPTER SEVEN

There were only two auto shops in the area around Greencreek. One was about ten miles further down Highway 78 and was part of a national chain business. The other was right in town, and it was named Stanford Auto. Sadie was pretty sure that was what Ginny said Ben's last name was, so it seemed like a safe guess that was the place she could find him. It was only a couple of blocks away. She set the destination in her GPS and arrived within minutes. Thankfully, the auto shop didn't look too busy. She knew she might not get in for an oil change right away, but she could schedule something and get a feel for the place—and hopefully, speak to Ben.

She opened the lobby door and stepped inside. The room held a cluttered front desk, three chairs, one of which was occupied by an older man reading a magazine, and stacks of tires and rims that took up the space along the walls everywhere else. The air smelled like grease and fresh rubber, and a blast of icy air conditioning wrapped around her.

A young woman was seated behind the desk. She looked up with a cheerful smile on her face and said, "Hi, welcome to Stanford Auto. How can I help you?"

"I was wondering if I could schedule an oil change for my SUV," Sadie said. "I'm almost due for one."

"No problem," the woman said. "We could probably even get you in right now if you have time. Have we helped you before?"

"No, I'm new to the area," Sadie said.

"Great. I'll get you set up with a rewards account. With every thousand dollars you spend, you get a free oil change, which can be a nice bonus if you have to get any bigger repairs done here. Can I have your name, your phone number, and your email address?"

Sadie recited her information and waited while the young woman typed it into the computer. While she was waiting, a door behind the counter opened, and a middle-aged man with salt-and-pepper hair and a neatly trimmed beard stepped out. He was wearing a dark blue service uniform that had the name *Ben* stitched on his right breast pocket.

Sadie was so focused on watching him get a drink of water from the cooler behind the counter that she missed whatever the young woman had said to her when she spoke again.

"I'm sorry," she said. "Could you repeat that?"

"I need to know the make, model, and year of your vehicle," she said. "I can come out with you to get the mileage when we're done here."

"Of course." She gave the young woman the information, but before she could stand up to go outside with Sadie, Ben came over and took the clipboard from her.

"I can get the rest of her information, Kelly. It's about time for your break, isn't it?"

"Are you sure?" she asked. "It'll only take a few minutes, I don't mind."

"It's a slow day today," Ben said. "She needs what, an oil change?" He glanced at the computer screen. "I'll take the vehicle straight back to bay two once I'm done getting the odometer reading."

Sadie followed him back outside and handed over the keys so he could record the number on the odometer. When he finished writing it down, he glanced into the back and spotted the live trap.

"What are you catching with that?" he asked. "Coyotes?"

"I'm trying to catch a lost dog," Sadie said. This was her chance to bring up Ginny. This *had* to be Ben Stanford—it would be way too much of a coincidence to have someone named Ben working at Stanford Auto otherwise. Not that it was impossible, but she would go with her gut on this one. "Virginia Kingsley's his owner. She actually mentioned you, which is why I decided to come here instead of going to that chain shop outside of town."

"Oh, Ginny sent you my way? You should have mentioned that, I'll have Kelly give you a discount. I heard about her husband. A shame, that. How'd you get dragged into helping her find their dog?"

"I run a boarding kennel at the motel on Highway 78," she explained. "He signed up for a beginner's dog training class that I was hosting. I think he was on the way there when the accident happened. When I heard Loki was missing, I volunteered to help out. I figured it was the least I could do."

"That's good of you," he said as he got out of her vehicle. "Have you spoken to Ginny? How does she seem to be holding up? I'm hoping she doesn't feel too guilty about what happened."

Sadie hesitated. It was clear that Ben knew Ginny

well—for one, he called her Ginny instead of Virginia, and he seemed genuinely concerned about her welfare. He wasn't acting suspiciously, per se, but if they were close, it raised the chances that he might fake an alibi for her or lie about her damaged vehicle.

"She was extremely upset when I saw her," Sadie said. "Why do you think she would feel guilty?"

"Oh, just because she's the one who asked him to take the dog to training," he said. "Michael was…" His expression twisted slightly as he paused, as if thinking about what to say. "He meant well, but he was bad at following through on things. I know she'd been complaining about the dog's behavior for weeks before she finally laid down the ultimatum for him. Then this happens." He shook his head. "I just know it's going to be tough for her, that's all."

That matched up with what Ginny told her, but the fact that her car mechanic knew about her marriage troubles raised a red flag. "What was Loki's behavior like? If I do manage to catch him, should I be worried about aggression?"

"Nothing like that." He shook his head. "The dog's rambunctious and has no manners, but he's not mean. Scratched me good by jumping up the last time I visited."

"Did you know the Kingsleys well?"

His expression grew closed off. "It's a small town," he said vaguely. "Can you run this clipboard back in to Kelly? I'll get your oil change started. Shouldn't be more than ten, fifteen minutes."

She accepted the clipboard from him and watched as he got back into her SUV and shut the door. She got the feeling there was something he was hiding—specifically, something about his relationship with Ginny.

CHAPTER EIGHT

Sadie decided to stop by Sunshine Desserts on her way home. She had already spent a lot of money today, between the cage and the oil change, but she wanted to get something to thank Sam for letting her borrow the trail cams, and she knew he liked their almond cookies. While she was paying for the cookie, she mentioned Loki to Bailey, the young woman who owned the little cookie shop, and Bailey revealed that she, too, had heard about the accident.

"The whole thing is just horrible," she said, as she handed Sadie the cookie in a little paper bag. "We get fatal accidents out here every once in a while—mostly drunk drivers or collisions with deer—but it's always a blow when it happens. Do you have any idea what caused the accident? I haven't heard anything solid yet."

"Nothing I can share," Sadie said. She paused, then decided to elaborate. She didn't want Bailey to think she was being rude, but she had promised she wouldn't spread rumors of a homicide around. She didn't want to lie, so she settled on a partial truth. "I'm helping his wife look for his dog, which was in the car when the accident happened, and I don't know how much she's ready to share yet."

"Got it," Bailey said. "Well, drive safely out there, and I hope you find that dog. If someone prints out flyers for him, I'm happy to hang one up here."

"That's a great idea," Sadie said. "I'll let Ginny know if I text her later today. I don't want to bother her too much since she just lost her husband. I bet Norma would let me hang a missing dog flyer up in the hardware store, too."

Bailey nodded. "I think most of the businesses in town would. Almost everyone likes dogs and no one wants to think of a pet being lost and alone in the wilderness."

It was something to think about if the live trap didn't work. Sadie said her goodbyes and headed back out to her SUV, where she set the cookie on the passenger seat and buckled up. She was planning to go straight to Wildermuth Road, but at the last moment she realized she didn't have anything to bait the trap with. They probably sold some cheap canned food at the hardware store, but she had already spent enough money today and she had a whole box of it at home. It wouldn't take her long to make a quick detour to the motel before going back out to Wildermuth Road.

Her first stop was Sam's house. She carried the little bag with the cookie in it up to his door and knocked, but there was no answer. When she looked around at the yard, she realized his truck wasn't there—he must be out. More disappointed than she expected, she went back to her vehicle to grab a scrap of paper and a pen. She wrote a note telling him the cookie was thanks for letting her borrow the trail cams, and left it tucked under a rock on the little table next to his porch furniture.

Leaving the cookie there for him to find, she drove the short distance to the motel, where she ran inside to grab a cheap metal dog bowl and a can of beef stew-flavored wet food from the kennel room. She paused to say hi to Jasper and the other dogs, and promised she would be back later for their walks, then said a hurried goodbye to Penny on her way out.

She didn't remember exactly where she saw Loki

run across the road, so she drove up and down Wildermuth Road for a few minutes until, through the trees, she spotted a gray sweatshirt hanging from a branch. She remembered Landon saying he would leave one there and decided that this must be the right spot. She pulled as far onto the shoulder as she could and left her hazards on when she got out to drag the heavy cage out of the back.

She carried it into the woods until it was just out of view of the road. She didn't want the already frightened dog to be spooked by passing cars or risk having someone see him if the trap caught him, and either take him or mess with him before she was able to get out here. She returned for the bag with the trail cameras in it, the bowl, and the can of food. She emptied the can into the bowl and placed it far at the back before setting the trap. She had no idea what she would do if she *did* catch a coyote or some other wild animal. Maybe Sam would help her set it free. It would be a good excuse to spend more time with him—not that she needed an excuse or wanted to spend more time with him…

She set up the trail cams next, one looking out over the trap so she could see whether the food lured Loki close even if he ended up not going into the cage, and the other she set up along a game trail a little deeper into the woods, since it seemed a likely path for him to take if he was heading toward the trap. She crinkled the paper bag up and picked up the empty can, taking both with her as she returned to her SUV.

She paused a few feet from the road when she saw a familiar stormy gray sedan parked behind her vehicle. Landon was getting out from the driver's side. He waved when he saw her.

"Any luck?" he called out.

"Not yet," she said. "I just set up a live trap and baited it with some canned dog food. I'll come back to check it this evening and then again in the morning. I'm hoping that will lure him out. Have you seen him since last night?"

"Nope," Landon said. "I left my sweatshirt like you suggested, and I came back early this morning to see if he was hanging around, but no luck."

"I saw," she said, nodding toward where the sweatshirt was hanging off a branch. "Do you think Ginny would be willing to part with one of her shirts or one of Michael's shirts? He might be a little more familiar with their scents these days."

Landon pressed his lips together. "I don't think he ever really bonded with them. He'll remember my smell. I got him as a little puppy. If he'll come to anyone, he'll come to me."

"Well, all right," Sadie said.

She didn't want to press the issue with him, and it wasn't as if she needed his permission anyway. If the live trap didn't work by tomorrow morning, she would text Ginny back to ask about the shirts and tell her about Bailey's suggestion. She didn't want to overwhelm her, but she did want to find Loki, and each day he was out here only increased the chances that he would get injured or eat something that made him sick.

"Let me give you my number," Landon said. He ducked back into his vehicle to grab his phone. "That way you can tell me if you find him."

"I already have Ginny's number," she said. "I'm sure she'd let you know."

"Well, I don't know if she'll want him back," Landon said. "Truth be told, I don't think she ever really wanted a dog, and I don't want him to end up in the pound. I'd really like to know when you get him, if that's okay."

She hesitated again, but she didn't know the circumstances of why he had rehomed his dog, and it wasn't as if she had to use his number, even if she had it. In the end, she agreed to exchange numbers with him. Once he had hers saved in his phone, he tucked his phone into his pocket and nodded toward the woods.

"I'm going to take another walk and see if I can find him," he said. "I might move my sweatshirt closer to wherever you set up that live trap too. Thanks again for helping out. I'll do whatever it takes to get this guy home."

He waited by his car until Sadie pulled away. She watched him in the rearview mirror, wondering if her suspicion of Ginny was misplaced. Maybe *Landon* had a motive to hurt Michael—just how badly did he want his dog back?

Or, he could just be a concerned person who wanted the best for Loki. Sadie had never rehomed a dog, but she imagined if she had to one day she would want to stay in touch with whoever adopted him, and if he ever got lost, she knew she would be out there looking just as hard as Landon was.

With a sigh, she started back toward the motel. All of this paranoia and suspicion was going to drive her crazy. She wished she could just focus on finding the dog and taking care of her duties at the motel, but even after Loki got home safely, she wouldn't be able to rest until she knew who had killed Michael Kingsley.

CHAPTER NINE

She was distracted by thoughts of Loki, Ginny, and Michael for the rest of the day, but she managed to get all of her chores done and spent a few hours in the lobby. Then she cleaned the room when the guests in Room Two checked out. She was happy to give Penny some time off. Her friend looked much more relaxed by the time she returned in the evening.

"You know, Greencreek isn't so bad," she said as she joined Sadie in the lobby. "There are a lot of nice people here."

Sadie narrowed her eyes, watching her friend suspiciously. "What happened? Did someone ask you out?"

Penny's cheeks turned pink, the color clashing with her hair. "Am I that obvious? Really?"

"I know you too well," Sadie said. "I know that look."

"I didn't say yes," Penny said. "I told him I'm not ready to date yet, and that I'm too busy focusing on building my business. But it was still nice to be asked. I…I think I might be close to being ready again. It's going to be hard to trust someone after what happened, but I don't want to go through my whole life alone."

"Who asked you?" Sadie asked. "Is it someone we know?" For a second, she wondered if it was Sam and felt a spike of irrational jealousy.

To her relief, her friend said, "I don't think you'd know him. He's the guy who works at the gas station. Not exactly a fancy job, but he seems nice enough. He gave me his number in case I changed my mind."

"I'm happy for you," Sadie said. "I think it'll be good for you to start dating again."

"What about you?" her friend asked, scooting the chair forward so she could rest her elbows on the desk and her chin in her hands. "Do you think you'll be ready to date soon, or have you sworn off all men forever?"

"Nothing that dramatic," Sadie said. "I just…I don't know if I want to start something when we don't even know if we'll be here in another six months."

"It's just dating," Penny said. "It's not like you have to marry the first guy you go out to dinner with. But yeah, I get it. That's why I said I wasn't ready yet, because everything is so up in the air. We're doing better, though. For a while there, I was worried I'd have to ask my parents for a loan."

Sadie wrinkled her nose. "You hate asking them for help."

"Yeah, I know," her friend said. "But I'd be willing to do it if it was the difference between us having to sell the motel and being able to keep it."

"Well, thankfully, I don't think things are that dire yet," Sadie said. "You're right, we are doing a little better. But we really need to get business up if we want to do more than scrape by every month."

"We'll get there," Penny said, with a certainty Sadie didn't feel. "I'll take over now, if you want. I'm just going to watch videos on my computer for a while. I don't think we'll get any more guests tonight, but who knows, maybe we'll get lucky."

"All right," Sadie said, rising from her chair, "I'm going to go take the dogs on their walks."

Walking the dogs through the twisting game paths on the ten acres of wooded land they owned always helped clear her mind. Nothing in her life was perfect, not really, but this came close. There wasn't much she loved more than being outside with a dog. She always enjoyed watching her boarding clients brighten up when they got to explore the wooded paths.

She walked Jasper last and took her time with him, letting him run around off leash until it started to get too dark to see—something that happened earlier now than it used to. The year was progressing, which might be a good thing. She held out hope that the holiday season would bring them more business. She brought Jasper into the lobby with her when she returned to the motel, and he trotted over to his water bowl in the corner to drink from it, splashing water over the sides.

Penny was watching a movie on her laptop, her feet propped up on the front desk. When Sadie came in, she looked up and said, "Your phone buzzed a couple of times. I didn't check it, so I don't know who it was, but I thought you'd want to know."

Sadie grabbed the device from where she'd left it next to her purse behind the front desk and found a couple of text messages from her mother, who wanted to know when she could come visit, and another from Sam. She ignored her mother's messages for now—she would call her later—and read the one from Sam.

Got the cookie. Thanks. You didn't need to, though. How'd your day go? Any luck with Loki?

Not yet, she typed. *I'm about to go out and check the live trap. Fingers crossed.*

It's getting dark out there, he typed back a second later. *Want some company?*

She bit her lip as she stared at his message. She felt bad about asking him to do so much, but this time she wasn't asking—he was offering. And it *would* be nice to have company, especially if she found Loki.

If you don't mind, I'd love some, she replied.

I'll be over in five.

"What are you smiling about?" Penny asked, narrowing her eyes as Sadie put her phone down.

"Nothing," Sadie said reflexively. Then she realized she was going to have to tell Penny that Sam was coming over, so she reluctantly admitted, "Sam's coming with me to check the live trap, that's all. He'll be here in a couple of minutes."

"I should have guessed," Penny said. She fluttered her eyelashes and made an exaggerated kissy face. "I knew I wasn't imagining things. You like him."

"Sam's a nice guy," Sadie said, neither denying nor confirming her friend's accusation.

Penny leaned back in her chair, crossing her arms.

"Right, the guy who nearly scared us to death with an axe when we first moved here is a nice guy."

"He is," Sadie said. "He thought we were breaking in, and he was just going to scare us away. You still don't like him very much, do you?"

Penny hesitated, her expression indecisive. "It's not that I dislike him, exactly," she said. "I just think it's kind of weird to have some random guy living in a house that's like a hundred feet from the motel. I didn't sign up to be a landlord." She shrugged. "I don't know, I don't think he's bad. It's a little strange trying to talk to someone who can't talk back, but I guess I'm getting used to it. I don't see why you like him so much, but I'm still happy for you. We've never had the same type anyway, which is probably a good thing."

"It's not his fault our real estate agent neglected to mention an entire house that came with a tenant," Sadie said, feeling defensive. "And there's nothing wrong with him being mute."

"I didn't say there was," Penny said. "It just makes it harder to get a feel for him. I'm saying he's not my type, that's all. I'm pretty sure he likes you, too. As long as he treats you right, that's really all that matters."

"I'll admit that I like him more than I probably

should, but I don't want you making a big deal about it or dropping hints to him," Sadie said. She grabbed her purse. "He's just a friend. You and I both agree that our focus is on the motel right now anyway, so it doesn't matter."

"If you say so," Penny said. "Do you think you'll be out late?"

"Not too late," Sadie said. "Why? Do you need me to grab you something from town?"

"I'm just thinking about what we should do for dinner."

"I can get something from the diner," Sadie said. "Text me what you want."

She raised a hand in farewell and stepped outside just in time to see Sam's flashlight as he made his way down the path between his house and the motel. She tried not to think too much about her discussion with Penny as she walked over to meet him. She didn't need to be distracted. They were out here to rescue a dog, nothing more.

And Sam didn't like her, not like that. He was being nice because he was their tenant, that was all.

CHAPTER TEN

She and Sam drove the short distance to Wildermuth Road in silence. This time, she kept her eyes peeled and her foot hovering over the brake, ready to stop her vehicle at the slightest sign of movement from the forest on either side, but she saw nothing, not even a deer.

She remembered the right spot to pull off at, at least, even though Landon's sweatshirt was gone. She remembered him saying he was going to move it, and it looked like he had, because she saw it hanging in a bush not far from the live trap.

The empty live trap. The food hadn't been touched yet, not even by a mouse or a chipmunk.

"Darn it," she muttered, disappointed. "I was hoping I'd have caught him by tonight."

Sam patted her shoulder in silent comfort, though he removed his hand quickly. She shot him a quick smile, then walked over to the trail cam. She had already hooked the app up to her phone, so it was just a matter of connecting her phone to the camera's bluetooth signal and downloading the images. There were only a few—she saw a deer wandering by, a squirrel that sniffed the food through the bars then decided it wasn't tasty enough to risk, and a couple of wild turkeys that ignored the trap completely.

Sam followed her out to the other trail camera, but this one hadn't captured anything but a rabbit hopping along the game trail. Disappointed, her shoulders slumped as they turned back toward the road.

"I hope he's safe somewhere," she said. "Maybe he'll wander closer to the trap overnight."

Sam typed out a message, the glow from his phone illuminating his front as they walked. He handed it to her to read.

The dog is lucky to have someone like you out here looking for him. I'm sure he'll be fine.

"Thanks," she said, glad he couldn't see the way her cheeks turned pink in the dark. Darn Penny. Sam was just being nice. "Do you mind if we swing by the diner?" she asked when they reached her SUV. "I told

Penny I'd pick up something for dinner on the way home."

He nodded and quickly typed out another message. *Do you want to sit down and eat? We can still bring her back something before we leave.*

Eating dinner with Sam—it almost sounded like a date, but she knew she was being ridiculous. It was just a meal between acquaintances. Friends? Yes, they were friends by now, or at least she thought they were. Either way, her stomach rumbled. She was hungry. She had eaten a late breakfast, then hadn't remembered to eat anything else, and taking all the dogs on their long walks had whetted her appetite.

"Sure, that sounds nice," she said after a moment's hesitation. "Penny will just have to wait a little bit longer for her food."

When they reached the diner, they seated themselves at a booth in the corner by the window. Sam didn't bother to look at the menu. He had been eating here his entire life and clearly already knew what he wanted. Sadie perused hers and settled on the chicken salad wrap she knew Penny liked to take home for her friend, and a plate of homemade lasagna with a house salad for herself. She hadn't had good, home-cooked comfort food in a long time. She really should start cooking more of her own meals, but it was hard to find the motivation when she was so stressed about the motel.

After she put in her order, making sure that Penny's would come in a to-go box, Sam fished his notebook out of his pocket to write down his own order; a burger and fries. He seemed to prefer writing by hand, though the phone was easier for him to manage in a moving vehicle.

Have you heard anything more about Michael's death? he wrote on a fresh page when the waitress left.

She shook her head. "Not yet." She paused and looked around to make sure no one was close enough to overhear. When she spoke again, she did so in a lowered voice, "Though I *did* talk to Ben Stanford. I took my SUV in for an oil change and managed to bring up the topic of Ginny and Michael. It was weird —he seemed to know Ginny very well. He even knew about her issues with Loki and her being the one to make Michael sign up for the training class."

I know Ben, Sam wrote. *He's done some work on my truck for me, and my old car before that. I know he was seeing someone a little while ago, but he kept quiet about who. I always wondered if it was a married woman.*

"You think she could have been Ginny?"

Sam shrugged and she frowned as she thought. It seemed possible, to her. Either Ben was a very close family friend of the Kingsleys, or there was something going on between him and Ginny.

"If he was seeing her, then that means he might have had a motive to kill Michael," she said.

She thought back to her visit to the auto shop, trying to remember if she had seen any damaged cars there, but if he had run someone off the road, he probably wouldn't have left the vehicle in question sitting out where anyone could see it. The car might even be fixed by now—he had the tools and supplies to do it himself, and without the evidence of a damaged vehicle, it would be hard to prove that he had done anything.

He seems like a good guy from what I know of him, Sam wrote. *But I could be wrong. How did he seem when you spoke to him?*

"He seemed very concerned for Ginny," she said. "But not nervous or suspicious or anything like that."

She fell silent as the waitress brought their food to them, with Penny's wrap packed away in a box to go. She took a bite of her lasagna, which was perfect—the cheese was melted and creamy, except for the top, which was crispy and golden brown, the sauce not too sweet, and the noodles were cooked perfectly. Sam took a bite of his burger, and they ate in silence for a few minutes until the worst of their hunger had abated.

You'll be careful? Sam wrote when he put his nearly finished burger down. *Poking around could be dangerous.*

"I am trying to be circumspect about it," she said. "My main priority is Loki. I know the sheriff is already working on the homicide case, and I'm sure he'll do a way better job than I could. I just can't help but wonder about it."

I don't want you to get hurt too, he wrote.

She smiled at him, touched, and took another bite of her lasagna. Penny didn't know what she was talking about. Sam was a good person, that was all. It was nice of him to worry about her, but she didn't need it. She would be fine.

CHAPTER ELEVEN

She woke early the next morning so she could finish her kennel chores before she went out to check on Loki. If he was in the trap, she didn't want to leave him out there too long. It would get hot soon, and there was always the chance that a human or another animal might bother him while he was trapped in the cage.

It was about an hour after sunrise when she left the motel. She wasn't going to bother Sam this early, so she simply told Penny where she was going and when she expected to be back, then set out for Wildermuth Road.

The live trap was empty when she reached it. Disappointed for the second day straight, she downloaded the photos from both trail cams, but she didn't check them right away. Beth was supposed to arrive with Rosco for his usual weekend stay, and she wanted to be there when she dropped him off so she could check on Rosco's progress with walking politely on a lead.

She paused when she got back to her SUV to text Ginny an update. She told her that she had set the live trap and checked it twice already with no results, then passed on Bailey's suggestion about printing out flyers, and ended the message by asking if Ginny would be willing to part with anything that smelled like her or Michael in the hopes that it might lure Loki in.

Ginny responded while she was driving back to the motel, and Sadie checked the message in the parking lot. *Absolutely, both of those sound like great ideas. You said you work at the motel on Highway 78, right? I can stop by in a little bit to drop the shirts off. Do you have a printer I could use for the flyers?*

Yes, and you're welcome to use it, Sadie typed back. *I should be available for the rest of the morning. If you text me a good picture of him, I can ask my friend to help me design some missing dog flyers for you.*

That was what she and Penny spent the next hour

doing, with a short break when Beth arrived with Rosco.

"He's doing great," Beth said when Sadie asked about his progress. "He's still not perfect, but I can tell he's improving already. Is there any chance you'd help me keep up with his training while he's here this weekend?"

"Absolutely," Sadie said.

Normally, she would charge more for a board and train, but she didn't feel right doing it so soon, especially not with Beth, who had been their very first regular client. She held a soft spot in her heart for the pair.

After she got Rosco settled in his kennel, she returned to help Penny finish designing the flyers. They printed off a sample by the time Ginny arrived. She was carrying a plastic bag, which she opened to show Sadie two flannel pajama shirts inside.

"I brought one from each of us," she said. She paused to gaze sadly at the red flannel. "I'd like to get both of them back, if that's okay with you. I have a hard time giving up anything of Michael's, but I know he would say it was worth it if it means getting Loki back."

"Of course," Sadie said. "If it's all right with you, I think I'll tuck them into the live trap, along with the bowl of dog food. They might get a little dirty, but that way nothing will be able to run off with them."

"Thank you," Ginny said. "Really, thank you so much for all your help. I did go out there to call for him just a little while ago, but that's the first time I've managed to get out there since the accident. I know it probably seems like I don't care much, but I do. It's just that I've barely been functioning."

"I understand," Sadie said. "I'm going to go check the trap again later this evening, and I'll drop off the shirts then. With any luck, we won't even need them. Here, we made this sample flyer for you. I put both your number and my number on it. I hope that's all right."

She handed the paper over to Ginny. It featured a photo of Loki with his ears perked up and his tongue lolling out of his mouth.

"It's perfect," Ginny said. "Would you mind printing out some more? I'll drop them off at a few of the businesses in town on my way back home."

"I'll get right on that," Penny said. "Do you think twenty will be enough for now?"

Ginny nodded, and Penny typed on the keyboard. After a second, the printer hummed to life. While the printer printed out the flyers, Sadie offered Ginny a bottle of water and a cookie.

"They're from Sunshine Desserts," she said. "We have a few different flavors, though I think we're out of chocolate chip. You can take one if you'd like, no charge."

"That's a very kind offer, but I don't know if my stomach is settled enough to eat," Ginny said. "I've hardly been able to keep anything down. I feel sick and guilty about everything that happened."

"No one could have known he was going to get into an accident on the way to class," Sadie said. "You did the right thing by suggesting he take Loki here. It's tough to live with a poorly behaved dog."

Jasper had been a menace when she first adopted him, and she hadn't been able to leave him home alone without him tearing up everything in reach. Thankfully, his behavior had improved quickly, but not everyone had the skills or knowledge to train their dogs themselves.

"It's not just that," Ginny said. She closed her eyes and took a deep breath before opening them. "I was having an affair."

She barely got the words out before she broke down sobbing. Penny's eyes widened and she met Sadie's gaze over Ginny's head, then scrambled for the box of tissues. Sadie stood frozen. She wasn't surprised about the affair, but she *was* surprised that

Ginny had told them. It must have been weighing on her something awful.

"I'm sorry, I shouldn't have said anything," Ginny managed to choke out after she blew her nose on the tissue Penny gave her. "It's been eating away at me ever since he passed. You must think I'm a horrible person."

Sadie couldn't stand the thought of infidelity, especially after what happened to her and Penny, but she couldn't bring herself to say that to the sobbing woman.

"Do something," Penny mouthed from behind Ginny. Her friend hated conflict and couldn't stand seeing people upset.

"I think you're hurt," Sadie said, choosing her words carefully. "And grieving. I can tell you cared about him."

"I did," Ginny said, her voice hoarse. "But I wasn't in love with him. He was my best friend, but the passion left our marriage a long time ago. I think the only reason we were still together was because it was what we were used to, and I think he would have said the same thing if you'd asked him. A part of me wondered if he would even care about the affair, but there's another part of me that's glad he never had to find out about it. Does that make me a monster?"

Sadie pressed her lips together, not sure what to say. She was pretty certain Michael would have rather learned about his wife's affair than end up murdered on the side of the road, but it didn't seem the appropriate thing to say to Ginny at the moment.

Penny must have seen her indecision because she cut in. "So, you were having an affair. Do you think your affair partner could be behind what happened?"

"Didn't the sheriff ask you not to tell anyone that Michael was murdered?" Ginny asked, with an accusatory look at Sadie.

"He didn't mean not to tell Penny," Sadie said. "I tell her everything."

"Yeah, I'm pretty sure the last time we kept secrets from each other was when I stole her nail polish in seventh grade."

Sadie rolled her eyes at her friend, but she couldn't argue—that had been one of their worst fights, but she had forgiven the slight a long time ago.

"Well, to answer your question," Ginny said. "No, Ben wouldn't do that. He's a sweetheart. He knew how much I cared for Michael, even if I wasn't in love with him anymore, and we had already talked about me leaving Michael to be with him. I just needed some time to figure things out first."

"What about Landon?" Sadie asked, eager to

move the conversation away from the topic of infidelity. "He seems very interested in getting Loki back. He suggested you might not want to keep him." She hesitated, then added, "He even asked for me to contact him first if I found Loki. I'm not going to do that, but it makes me worry that he might be up to something."

"Oh, he's texted a few times over the past few years asking for his dog back, but he was always very polite about it. He's a nice young man. He just went through a rough patch a while ago. There were a few times I might have agreed to return Loki, but Michael loved that dog to death, and Loki felt the same way about him. The two would have been miserable if they split up, and Landon knew that." Her expression grew even more serious. "And I definitely want Loki back. He's the last living piece I have of my husband. It might take some time, but I know we can bond with each other, and I couldn't stand the thought of him going anywhere else. I'll even take him to training here, like Michael was going to, if you're all right with me waiting a few months until my life is a little more under control. Would you be willing to apply whatever he paid you to my lessons?"

"Of course," Sadie said. "If you want the money back now, I'll return it to you, and you can sign up for classes later at the same price." It would be a blow, but it was the right thing to do.

"No, no," Ginny said. "You keep it. It'll encourage me to actually take Loki to the lessons. I just hope he's okay. You haven't seen him at all since the day of the accident?"

"No—" She broke off, remembering that she hadn't checked the cameras yet. "Actually, let me take a look at the pictures I downloaded from the trail cameras. He didn't go into the trap, but he might have approached it. Dogs can be wary of new things sometimes, especially when they're in a scary new environment like Loki is."

While Ginny waited, Sadie pulled out her phone and loaded the app where she had downloaded the photos from the trail cams. She checked the furthest one first, but there was nothing except for a few robins and a deer. She checked the one that looked out over the trap next. A couple of raccoons had come sniffing around the cage during the night, but something scared them off. The next picture was of a white blur. She quickly swiped. The next image was of Loki sniffing the entrance of the trap. And the next showed him inside of it. After that, she saw multiple pictures of the dog trapped in the cage and could only stare, utterly confused because the cage had been not only empty, but propped open and reset when she arrived.

"What is it?" Ginny asked. "Do you see him?"

"Just a second," Sadie said.

She kept swiping until, in the gray light of dawn, she saw a person appear on the screen. Landon. He didn't seem aware of the security cameras, but she saw him look around before he let the dog out of the cage. The last photo showed him walking away with a leash around Loki's neck. She had arrived half an hour later… if only she had gone out to check the trap before she took care of the boarding dogs, she would have been the one to find him.

"What happened? Is he hurt?" Ginny asked.

Sadie held the phone out to her. "He's not hurt, but I think he was stolen."

CHAPTER TWELVE

"He took Loki, and he didn't tell either of us?" Ginny asked. She was still flipping back and forth through the pictures, as if she expected them to change. "I don't understand. Why would he do that?"

"He wanted the dog back," Sadie said. "I guess he didn't realize I'd set up the trail cams. I should have told him. It might have discouraged this."

"Or he would have just taken the trail cams too," Ginny said. She handed the phone back to Sadie; her face flushed with anger. "He stole my dog. I'm going to go get him back. I still remember where he lives."

"Hold on a second," Sadie said. "Maybe we can get him to admit that he has Loki. If we ask him whether he's seen the dog, he might come clean."

Ginny scowled, but said, "It's worth a try. You're

going to have to call him. I don't think I can talk to him without giving him a piece of my mind."

"I feel like I should make popcorn for this," Penny said. "I didn't expect this to end in dog theft. You're lucky Sam gave you those cameras, or you might never have known."

Lucky indeed. She would have to find a better way to thank him later. First, they needed to get Loki back. Regardless of her personal feelings about Ginny's affair, she was Loki's rightful owner.

"I'm going to call him now," she said, pulling up the contacts list on her phone. "Neither of you say anything."

Penny mimed zipping her lips, and Ginny nodded. Sadie dialed Landon's number. He answered after just a couple of rings.

"Hello?"

"Hey, Landon," Sadie said. "I was wondering if you've had any luck with Loki yet. If you've seen even a hint of him out there in those woods, I could move the cage closer to his current location. I went out to check it again this morning, but there was nothing."

Landon was silent for a long second... so long, she was almost certain that he was about to come clean. However, in the end, he didn't.

"Sorry, I haven't seen him," he said. "I'll keep looking, though."

She thanked him as politely as she could and ended the call. When she hung up, she shook her head. "He's not giving anything up."

"That's it," Ginny said. "I'm going to get my dog back."

"By yourself?" Sadie said. "Shouldn't we, I don't know, call the police or something?"

"I always heard that possession is nine-tenths of the law," Ginny told her. "And I'm sure he still has some of Loki's old vet records. What if they side with him and say he can keep Loki? Michael was the one who owned him, technically, and he's gone now. I can't take the risk. I'm sure Landon will give him back if I show up there asking for him."

Ginny snatched up the stack of flyers and left the lobby in a hurry. Sadie stared after her.

"This is a terrible idea. She shouldn't be going there alone."

"We could call Sheriff Islington," Penny suggested.

"I don't know if that's the right thing to do," Sadie said. "She might be right. Dogs are treated like property in a lot of cases, and who knows what proof of ownership Landon might have. It could get messy."

"What are you doing?" Penny asked of Sadie as she took her purse out from behind the front desk.

"I'm going to go with her," she said. "That way if something goes wrong, at least I'll be able to call for help."

Penny gave a long-suffering sigh. "Of course you are. If you end up getting murdered or kidnapped, I'll take care of Jasper for you."

"Thanks," Sadie said dryly. "I'll let you know when I'm on my way back."

She slipped her phone into her purse and took her keys out of it, then hurried out through the lobby door to catch up with Ginny.

Ginny was a woman on a mission. She didn't mind Sadie coming with her, but she wasn't waiting around for anyone, so Sadie ended up following behind her in her SUV. She managed to keep up with the other woman, barely, and pulled up behind her when she turned into the driveway of a small house a few blocks away from Main Street.

Landon's car was parked in front of the garage, but another vehicle was next to it, this one covered by a tarp. Sadie itched to go peek under the tarp and see whether the second vehicle had damage consistent with running someone off the road, but Ginny was already marching up to the front door.

She reached the front stoop just as Ginny knocked on the door. Well, not knocked, exactly. Pounded. She kept pounding on the door without pause, relentlessly, until Landon pulled it open. Somewhere inside, a dog was going crazy barking at them.

Sadie saw him peek out. As soon as he spotted Ginny, he slammed the door in her face, and she heard the deadbolt turn.

"I know you have Loki in there!" Ginny shouted through the door. "Bring him out right now, or I'm coming back with Michael's shotgun. You have no right to steal my dog from me, especially not right after I lost my husband."

There was no response. After a pause, Ginny continued shouting.

"Landon, I'm not joking around. Bring him out this instant or you'll be sorry."

"Ginny, maybe we should call the police after all," Sadie said. "I don't think he's going to give Loki up, no matter how much you threaten him."

"Oh, he will," Ginny said. She kicked the door. "I'm going to make him. That's my dog you've got in there, you—"

She broke off as the deadbolt turned again and Landon yanked the door open. Ginny was opening her mouth for another tirade when she screamed instead and jumped backward just as a baseball bat smashed through the air right where her head had been.

Sadie jumped back with a shriek of her own and reached for her purse and her pepper spray, but she had left it in her SUV. She couldn't believe she'd made that sort of mistake, but she had been in a hurry to catch up with Ginny. She grabbed Ginny's arm and hauled her back just as Landon made a second swing. Her eyes caught on a stain on the wooden bat—something dark at the tip of it. Blood? It looked like it had been cleaned, but whatever it was had stained the wood deeply.

Landon's face was red as he took another step toward Ginny. He barely seemed to see Sadie. His entire focus was on the woman in front of him. Ginny kept stumbling back until she tripped and went sprawling on the grass. Sadie jumped forward, hoping to grab Landon's arm or maybe the bat, but he turned it on her, catching her with a glancing blow across the ribs and knocking the breath out of her. She stumbled back and watched in horror as Landon raised the bat over Ginny.

But the barking was getting closer, as if the dog had broken out of wherever it had been locked up, and just before Landon started his downward swing,

Loki came out of the house like a missile and latched on to Landon's calf.

Landon screamed and spun around. He tried to haul Loki off by his collar at first, and when that didn't work, he gripped the bat in both hands. For a horrible second, she thought he was going to hit the dog, but he didn't. He just used the handle end of it to pry Loki's jaws apart. When the dog finally let go, he tossed the bat away and grabbed him by the collar.

"What was that for?" he shouted. "You're my boy. You love me. Why would you bite me?"

Ginny scrambled back on her hands and knees, and Sadie helped her rise to her feet. As soon as Ginny was standing on her own, Sadie let go of her so she could dart over to grab the bat. She was almost certain that stain on the end was blood. Landon must have seen her looking at it because he stopped talking to Loki. Still holding onto the dog's collar, he looked over at Sadie.

"Give that back."

"Are you kidding me?" she asked. "No way am I giving it back. You just tried to kill Ginny."

"He tried to bash my head in," Ginny said. "Just like…" She paused. "Just like Michael."

Landon's jaw clenched. Sadie didn't know if he was going to admit to anything or not, but it didn't matter. Not really. She had already put the pieces together. The bat was probably the only piece of evidence anyone would need, but she backed away from him and turned toward the covered vehicle in the driveway. She had to be sure.

"Hey, where are you going?"

She ignored him and carefully lifted the tarp that covered the vehicle. It was an old pickup truck, and the front right corner of it was crumpled in.

Ginny was staring at her, a question in her eyes. Sadie gave a single nod. This time it was Ginny who lashed out without warning. She dove at Landon, who somehow managed to keep hold of Loki's collar even while the woman was slapping at him.

"You did it. You killed my husband! All to get your dog back? You're a monster. How could you do that to Michael? And Loki—you know how much they loved each other."

"Quit it," he snapped, trying to shove her away. "Loki's my dog. He's not just a pet, he's family. I never should have sold him to Michael, and you should have given him back when I asked. I tried to handle it nicely, but you don't know what it's like to be separated from something you love."

"I don't?" Ginny shrieked. "I don't know what it's

like to be separated from something I love? My husband is dead because of you, you murderer!"

She managed to get him across the face, and he had to let go of the dog's collar to defend himself. Loki ran around barking until Sadie managed to snag him by the collar. She was a little afraid he was going to turn his teeth on her with all the excitement, but he just looked over his shoulder at her, then sat down, wagging his tail and panting.

"Come on, buddy, let's get you in the car," she said.

She hurried him over to her SUV and had him hop up in the back, where he sniffed Jasper's pile of blankets. She slammed the door shut, then got her purse off the front seat and scrambled for her phone. She glanced over at Landon and Ginny. She wasn't sure which of them was winning the fight, but at least it didn't look like they were in the process of killing each other. Shaken, she dialed 911.

She loved dogs as much as anyone—probably more than most people, in fact—but while she might have had sympathy for Landon's circumstances if things were different, murder wasn't ever something she would be okay with.

EPILOGUE

"Very good, everyone! You've all made a lot of progress. Your next homework assignment is to practice sit-stays. This will continue to help your dogs build their impulse control. Keep working on that loose-leash walking, too."

She gathered up the empty water bottles as her clients started to leave. Beth lingered to help with cleanup and chat. Rosco was a little better behaved than usual as he followed her around on his leash.

"I hope you know how grateful everyone is for these classes," she said. "The next closest dog trainer is almost an hour away. I know there isn't much here in Greencreek, but we really needed someone like you. I hope you'll stick around for a good long while."

"I hope so, too," Sadie said. "We don't plan to leave any time soon, at least not as long as we can make ends meet with the motel."

"Well, my fingers are crossed that it will be a success for you," Beth said. "I know Rosco would be sad if you had to leave."

She bent down to pat her happy, energetic dog, and Sadie smiled at the sight. Working with dogs was a business for her, but it was also something she would have done for fun, even if she was a millionaire. There wasn't much she loved more than seeing people's bond with their pets grow and witnessing a dog's world open up once it learned some basic manners.

She walked Beth to the parking lot and waved goodbye, then stepped into the lobby, where she found Penny on the phone. She let Jasper go to drink out of his water bowl, then leaned against the counter.

"Absolutely. You'll get daily updates, and I think she offers extra updates for just a couple dollars more a day," Penny said. "They'll get a nice long walk once a day, and they'll have full access to the outdoor runs as well. Plus, Sadie's in and out of the kennels all day, so they'll get plenty of attention. We also have security cameras in each kennel, so she can check on the dogs even if she isn't in the room with them."

She paused while the person on the other end of the line spoke. "Great," she said after a second. "I have you down for five days at the beginning of November."

She said goodbye and ended the call, then turned to Sadie. "You just got two new boarding clients," she said. "They're from all the way up in Michigan: a pair of German Shepherds. I guess their owner's coming down here for some sort of convention, and she wants to bring her dogs down with her. I think she said it was a dental convention."

"That'll help, for sure," Sadie said. Two dogs for five nights wouldn't make them rich, but it would pay for most of next month's electricity bill.

"See?" Penny said. "Things are getting better. We just have to keep chugging along. One day, we'll look back on all of this and wonder why we were ever so worried about keeping the motel afloat. I just know it."

Printed in Dunstable, United Kingdom